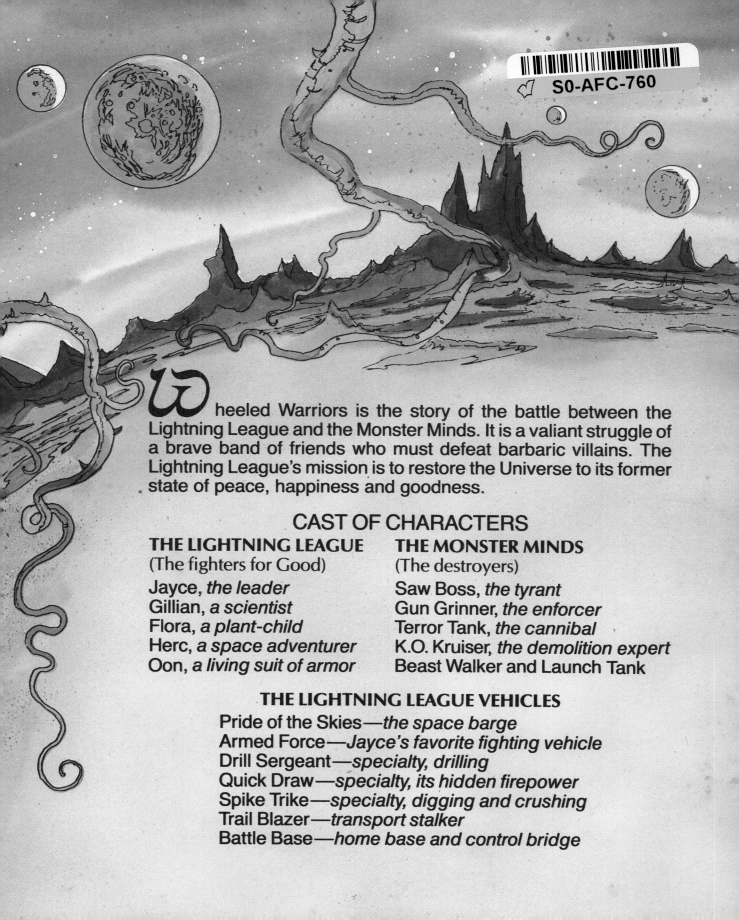

ω heeled Warriors is the story of the battle between the Lightning League and the Monster Minds. It is a valiant struggle of a brave band of friends who must defeat barbaric villains. The Lightning League's mission is to restore the Universe to its former state of peace, happiness and goodness.

CAST OF CHARACTERS

THE LIGHTNING LEAGUE
(The fighters for Good)

Jayce, *the leader*
Gillian, *a scientist*
Flora, *a plant-child*
Herc, *a space adventurer*
Oon, *a living suit of armor*

THE MONSTER MINDS
(The destroyers)

Saw Boss, *the tyrant*
Gun Grinner, *the enforcer*
Terror Tank, *the cannibal*
K.O. Kruiser, *the demolition expert*
Beast Walker and Launch Tank

THE LIGHTNING LEAGUE VEHICLES

Pride of the Skies—*the space barge*
Armed Force—*Jayce's favorite fighting vehicle*
Drill Sergeant—*specialty, drilling*
Quick Draw—*specialty, its hidden firepower*
Spike Trike—*specialty, digging and crushing*
Trail Blazer—*transport stalker*
Battle Base—*home base and control bridge*

WHEELED WARRIORS™

SEEDS OF BATTLE

A GOLDEN BOOK
Western Publishing Company, Inc.
Racine, Wisconsin 53404

Library of Congress Catalog Card Number: 85-070077
ISBN 0-932631-12-6

A B C D E F G H I J

Once this was a great city. It had been on this planet for many hundreds of years. Its people were healthy and happy.

Now the city was in ruins. It had become a place for weeds to grow over crumbling walls. No longer did the voices of happy people sound in the streets. The citizens of this place had left their world in spaceships. For this city was no longer theirs. It now belonged to the terrible Monster Minds!

Saw Boss, the leader of all the Monster Minds, rolled through the ruins. His three top henchmen, Gun Grinner, K.O. Kruiser and Terror Tank, followed him.

"This planet is ideal for us Monster Minds," said Saw Boss with a cruel smile. "Its soil is perfect for growing more of our kind. When enough of us have grown, we will spread through the whole universe. And no one will be able to stop us!"

K.O. Kruiser used his wrecking ball to scatter the seeds across the soil. These were the same kinds of seeds that produced the original Monster Minds. Then Saw Boss energized the seeds with a powerful growth ray.

"Uh, when do they start growing?" asked K.O. Kruiser. He was not the smartest Monster Mind in the group.

"Be patient!" snarled Terror Tank. "Keep tossing seeds!"

The smile on Saw Boss' face widened as something in the soil moved. Within moments, weird plants rose from the ground. They were growing fast and twisting into familiar shapes.

"Amazing!" said Gun Grinner. "Soon we'll have a new army."

"They will need time to become fully grown," said Saw Boss. "Then they will be mine to command. But just think, not a single human remains on this planet!" He laughed.

But this world still had *one* human inhabitant.

Old Skragg, the hermit, had refused to go away with his people. This was Skragg's home. It would always be home to him.

Skragg frowned. He vowed that someday, somehow, these plant creatures would be defeated. And on that day, the planet would again belong to his people.

Skragg slipped away unnoticed by the Monster Minds. He hurried to the old radio he had found in the ruins of his city. The radio had been damaged, though. Its power was running low. But Skragg had to risk trying to send a message for help.

He switched on the radio. It made a low humming sound that he hoped the Monster Minds did not hear. He directed the transmitter into space. "Can anyone hear me?" he said.

The radio signals traveled
through space. They reached
the old barge ship, the Pride
of the Skies. The battered
ship's name was almost a joke.
But there was one person
who was proud of the bulky old
craft. That was the ship's
captain, Herc Stormsailor.

The ship was also the
space-traveling headquarters
of Jayce and the Lightning
League, and their Battle Base.

A weak voice came through crackling static over the radio of the Battle Base. The voice was too weak for Jayce to identify. But its meaning was clear.

"Help me," said the voice. "Monster Minds!"

"I wonder," said Jayce, "could that be my father?"

Gillian paused, thinking before he answered. "It is possible, Jayce. But we must be careful—if it *isn't* Audric."

"Hey," said Herc, "listen to the radio on your own time. Remember, I still haven't been paid for joining your little club."

"You will be paid—someday," smiled Gillian, as he turned up the volume on the radio.

Suddenly, in a burst of static, the radio voice stopped. "What happened?" asked Jayce, worried.

Terror Tank had rolled in swiftly. He grabbed Skragg's radio and bit into it. "I've always had a special taste for radios," he said, munching.

"So," said Saw Boss, "there is still one human left."

"What should we do with him?" asked Gun Grinner, rolling to attention like a loyal sergeant.

"We'll find some use for him!" laughed Saw Boss.

Skragg's hands were bound and he was led away. The old man felt utterly helpless. All hope of saving his planet had gone.

As they passed the field of growing Monster Minds, K.O. Kruiser spoke. "Why don't we make our prisoner work in our fields."

"I was about to say that," said Saw Boss.

The group paused and looked toward the field.

The new Monster Mind plants were growing fast. Within minutes, they were looking more like the original Saw Boss, Terror Tank, Gun Grinner and K.O. Kruiser. Soon they would be fully grown, and they would have their own powerful weapons.

"When they have finished growing, we will plant more seeds," said Saw Boss. "Then this world will be overrun by our kind. And one more planet will be added to our empire!"

At that same time, Jayce was using the computers in the Battle Base. The computers traced the radio signal to its source. As Herc guided the Pride of the Skies toward the planet, Jayce's ring glowed. This was the very ring that had once belonged to Jayce's father.

"The ring is trying to tell me something," said Jayce. "Gillian, what do you think it means?"

"That is only for *you* to decide," Gillian said to Jayce. "Remember, the ring only responds to *you.*"

Jayce thought for a few moments. "It must mean we're going to the right place," he said. "I hope it also means that my dad sent the radio message."

"Hang on!" said Herc, working the ship's controls. "We're moving into the planet's orbit."

15

After Herc put the ship into orbit, Jayce released the Battle Base. The big vehicle was another of Gillian's inventions. It lowered on anti-gravity waves.

Jayce was getting more excited. If it was really Audric's voice on the radio, his quest would be over. Then he and his father could bring together two special plant roots and defeat the Monster Minds.

The Battle Base touched ground. Then it started to roll across the rough landscape.

Gillian worked the vehicle's computers. They lit up with scientific symbols. "According to the computers," said Gillian, "this world was once inhabited by humanoids. But now there is only a slight trace of humanoid life here. It must be the person who sent the message."

But the computers could not locate the humanoid's exact location.

Little Flora, the girl born from a flower, smiled. "Maybe I can help," she said. Flora looked at Brock, the flying fish created by Gillian. She concentrated hard and sent him a telepathic message—a message from her mind. Brock happily flew out of his bowl and through an opened window.

Brock, who was Flora's pet, made the perfect spy. He was small enough to watch things without being noticed.

Like an eagle, Brock flew away from the Battle Base. He soared over the strange terrain. His sharp eyes looked for anything that might be important. For a long time, he searched. Then he spotted the ruins of the city. He swooped down for a closer look.

Brock was astonished. Below him was the field of growing Monster Minds. He flew down lower, always keeping a safe distance away from the ugly crop.

Then he heard laughter that chilled him. He could see Saw Boss laughing with glee. And he saw that Terror Tank, Gun Grinner and K.O. Kruiser guarded a humanoid captive. Now, if only Brock could fly away without being seen...

Returning to the Lightning League Battle Base, Brock went right to Flora. Only she could understand the flying fish.

Excited, Brock made his whistling noises. That was how he made Flora understand him.

"The Monster Minds are growing more of their kind," said Flora. "They're in the ruins of a big city. And they have a prisoner. An older man. Maybe it's Audric !"

"So, what next?" asked Herc.

"I have a plan," said Jayce. "You, Oon and I will go out in Trail Blazer and drive to the ruins. Trail Blazer is big and powerful enough to protect us all from the Monster Minds."

"You want...m-me to go along, too?" asked Oon. His armored suit was rattling. "Won't I just get in the w-way?"

"My fee has just gone up, kid," said Herc.

As usual, Herc mellowed and went along with Jayce. Even Herc had to admit that Jayce really knew how to take charge. Maybe that was why Herc stayed this long with the Lightning League without being paid.

Trail Blazer, the big Stalker vehicle, soon rumbled over the rugged land. Jayce used the Stalker's weapons to clear away all obstacles in the way. They were almost at their goal.

23

At the fields, Saw Boss was too busy watching the plants' growth to hear the distant sound of Trail Blazer.

Jayce gunned the Stalker. He pushed it up to top speed. Trail Blazer sped over rocky ruins, with Drill Sergeant on board for any emergency. At last, Saw Boss heard the roar of mighty engines.

"The Lightning League!" growled Saw Boss. "They've found us—even here!"

"Now," said Jayce, "it's time to put my plan into action. Herc, take the controls. Oon, come with me! And bring a brain container!"

Oon was not the bravest member of the Lightning League, but when duty called, he answered. He followed Jayce out of the Stalker. In one hand, Oon carried the container. In the other, he dearly held the lance that he believed was magic.

There was only one way to make a Monster Mind helpless—take away its brain power. Jayce heroically leaped onto Saw Boss. Seconds later, Jayce pried open the canopy and wrestled out the plant brain!

The Saw Boss vehicle slowed down and stopped.

Jayce looked around. He saw no sign of any humanoid. The other Monster Minds must have hidden him, he thought. Then Jayce put the captured brain into the container.

"We'll have to look for the man somewhere else,"
Jayce told Oon. They were both running back toward
Trail Blazer. "But first, let's get this brain back to our
Battle Base."

"What if Saw Boss starts up again?" said Oon. "What
if he comes after us?"

"Without his brain, he can't move," said Jayce.

Trail Blazer was already far away when Terror Tank, Gun Grinner and K.O. Kruiser arrived on the scene.

"Saw Boss' brain has been captured!" said Gun Grinner. "That makes *me* the new leader of the Monster Minds!"

"No!" growled Terror Tank. "Saw Boss has always been our leader. He always will be! We must rescue his brain and put it back where it belongs!" He started planning a rescue mission.

28

Inside the Lightning League Battle Base, Jayce watched as Gillian studied Saw Boss' brain. "Can you make it tell us where they hid their human prisoner?" asked Jayce.

"I'm afraid not," said Gillian. "But maybe Flora can."

Flora concentrated hard. She tried using her mental telepathy on the brain. Then she shook her head. "All he says is that we'll be sorry if we don't let him go."

At that same time, Gun Grinner was putting his own plan into action. First, he ordered that the prisoner be held tightly. He shot an energy bolt which made some vines move. They crawled like serpents and wrapped themselves around Skragg.

Skragg tried to get free, but failed.

"The more you struggle," laughed Gun Grinner, "the tighter the vines will grab you. Now—let's get that brain!"

Flora kept on trying, but Saw Boss' brain refused to tell her any more. Jayce was ready to start another search for the man that might be his father. Suddenly the Battle Base shook.

"What's that?" said Herc. "A planetquake?"

"If only it were something as simple as that!" said Jayce. "The Monster Minds are attacking us!"

"We must defend ourselves!" said Jayce.
Terror Tank, Gun Grinner and K.O. Kruiser shot powerful beams toward the Battle Base. The Battle Base fired its own defensive rays. Sometimes those rays canceled out those fired by the enemy.

"If we can keep this up," said Herc, "maybe they'll just give up and go away. Awww, who am I kidding?"

The battle got worse.

"Why waste all this time and energy?" roared Terror Tank. "Saw Boss showed his weakness by letting his brain get captured. It's time I—Terror Tank—became your leader!"

"No!" growled K.O. Kruiser. His voice sounded over the noises of lasers. "Our leader will always be Saw Boss!"

But Terror Tank had already thought of a way to end the battle.

Leaving the scene of battle, Terror Tank sped to the fields where the crops were still growing. "Maybe," he thought, "the new Monster Minds are big enough to join the fight." He shot a ray over the field, getting the new vehicles' attention.

"Saw Boss needs your help now!" Terror Tank yelled.

Without delay, the new Monster Minds pulled themselves out of the ground. They started their brand new engines.

Like the leader he thought himself to be, Terror Tank sped away from the field. The young Monster Minds followed him.

The new Monster Minds obediently rolled into the battle. For the first time, they spun the young buzz saws. They swung the new wrecking balls and fired their rays. But because they were not yet fully grown, their weapons were not at full strength. Still, they fought hard.

35

The Battle Base resisted the attack of the new Monster Minds. Its tough hull withstood their weapons. It shot lasers at the ground, throwing up great clumps of dirt. And it flashed beams that scared the young vehicles, forcing them back.

"We're beating them!" exclaimed Herc.

"Let's regroup, warriors," shouted Gun Grinner. And the new fighters tried to obey their leader's orders.

Because the new Monster Minds were drained of their energy, their power left them, and they began to wither away. Soon they were no more than dried up weeds, then the weeds crumbled to dust.

Terror Tank still had a plan in his crafty brain. Again, he steered away from the battle, leaving Gun Grinner and K.O. Kruiser to fight by themselves.

Quickly, Terror Tank returned to the ruins. He grabbed Skragg and forced him to go to the combat zone.

From the Battle Base, Jayce saw the man. He yelled, "Stop firing!" Then Jayce realized that the man was not his father, but he knew he had to save the prisoner.

"Care to make a trade?" shouted Terror Tank. "This humanoid—for the brain of Saw Boss?"

"Saw Boss would like that," said Flora, getting another mental message from the brain. "But can we trust him?"

"It seems we have no choice," said Jayce.

"A wise decision," said Gillian. But the scientist could see the look of disappointment on the youth's face. "Don't worry, Jayce. You will find your father someday. I know you will."

Jayce and the Lightning League stepped out of the Battle Base. When the hermit was released from the vines, Jayce returned the brain to the other Monster Minds.

"We're safe for a while," said Jayce. "It will take them some time to put back Saw Boss' brain."

"Yeah," said Herc, as the Monster Minds drove away. "But after they're done, you can bet they'll be back!"

Jayce agreed. Within minutes, they were all inside the Pride of the Skies speeding through space.

"We will take you to your people," Jayce promised Skragg. "Thank you," the old man said, smiling.

"You can count on the Lightning League," said Jayce. "Remember our motto: *'A Courageous Heart, A Righteous Quest!'*"

0 74299 09849